D1387183

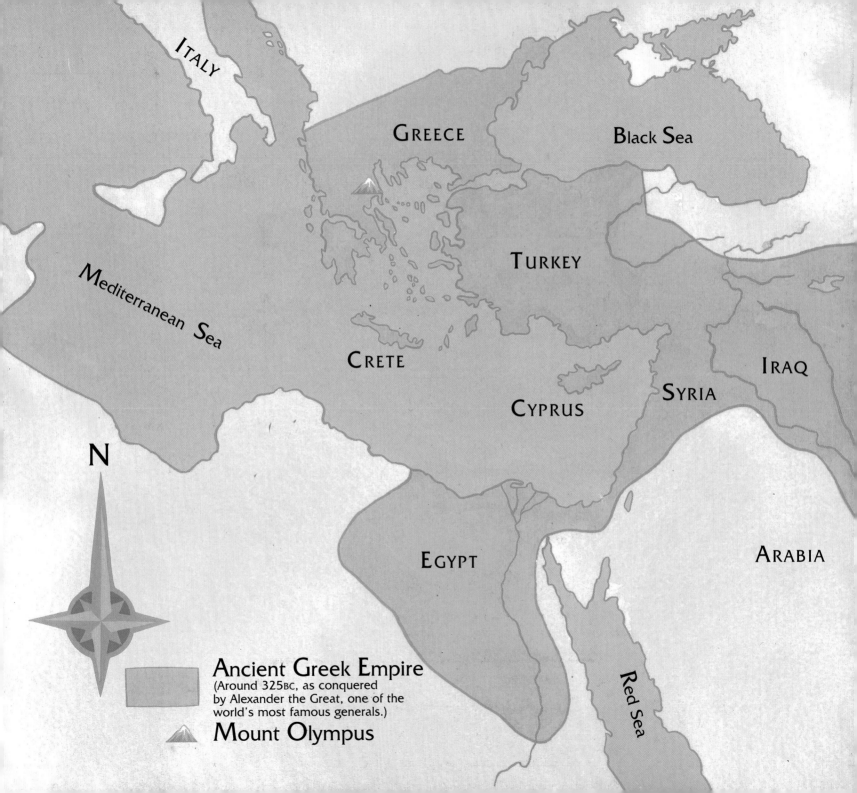

ITALY

GREECE

Black Sea

TURKEY

Mediterranean Sea

CRETE

CYPRUS

SYRIA

IRAQ

N

EGYPT

ARABIA

Red Sea

Ancient Greek Empire
(Around 325BC, as conquered
by Alexander the Great, one of the
world's most famous generals.)

Mount Olympus

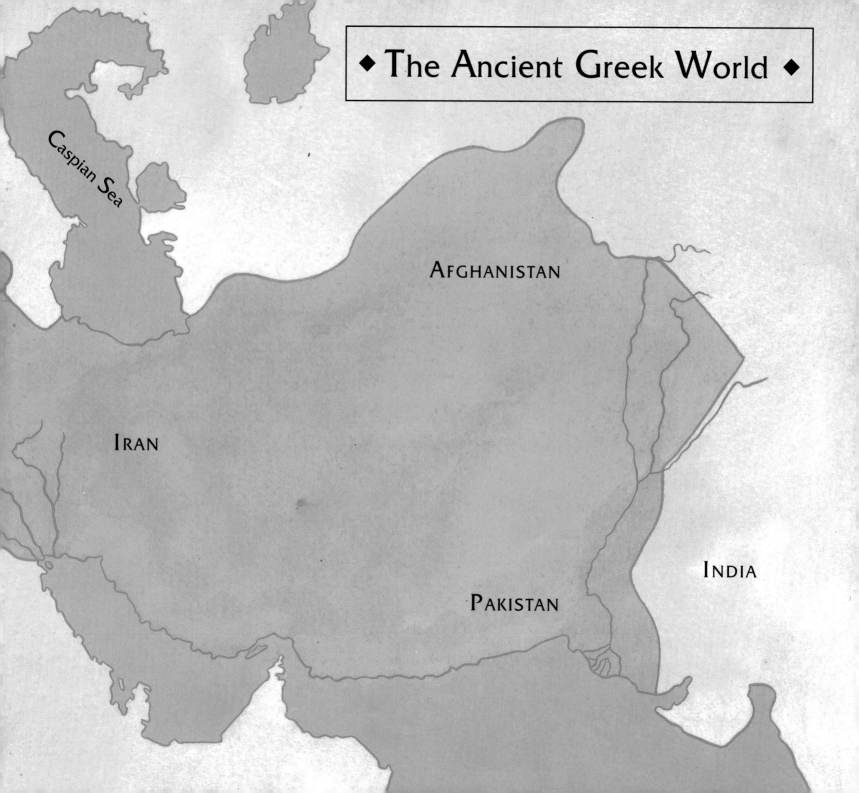

◆ The Ancient Greek World ◆

Caspian Sea

AFGHANISTAN

IRAN

INDIA

PAKISTAN

First published in Great Britain in 1999
This edition published in 2000
by Macdonald Young Books,
an imprint of Wayland Publishers Ltd

Macdonald Young Books
61 Western Road
Hove
East Sussex
BN3 1JD

Find Macdonald Young Books on the
internet at: http://www.myb.co.uk

Text © Sally Grindley 1999
Illustrations © Nilesh Mistry 1999

Editor: Rosie Nixon
Designer: Miriam Yarrien

© Macdonald Young Books 1999

Grindley, Sally
Pandora and the mystery box. - (Magical myths)
1.Pandora (Greek mythology) - Juvenile fiction 2.Legends
3.Children's stories
I.Title 823.9'14 [J]

ISBN 0 7500 2698 7

All rights reserved

Printed in Hong Kong by Wing King Tong

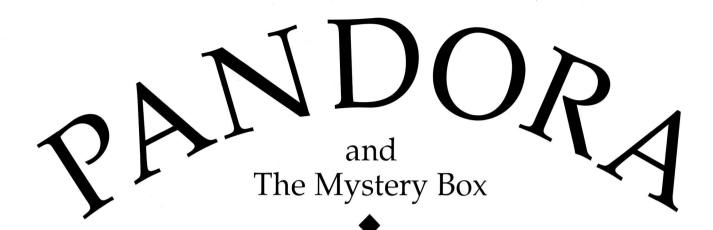

PANDORA

and
The Mystery Box

◆

Written by Sally Grindley
Illustrated by Nilesh Mistry

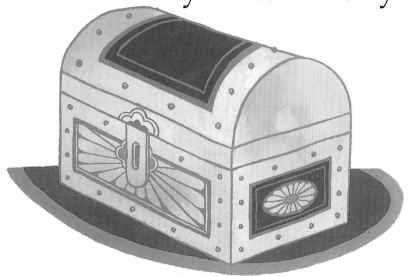

MACDONALD YOUNG BOOKS

FALKIRK COUNCIL
LIBRARY SUPPORT
FOR SCHOOLS

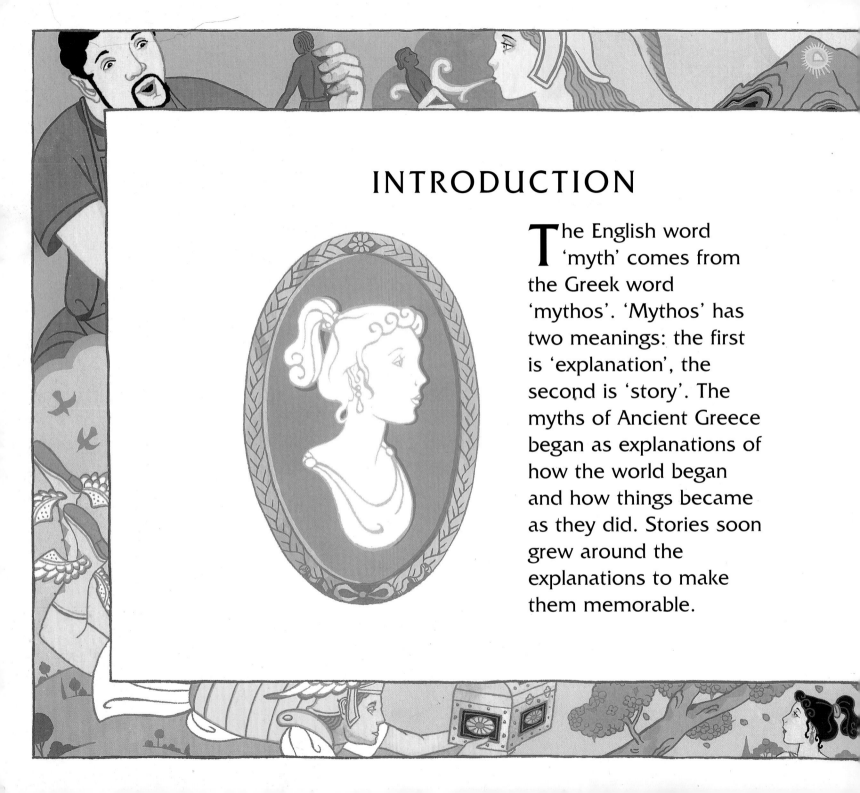

INTRODUCTION

The English word 'myth' comes from the Greek word 'mythos'. 'Mythos' has two meanings: the first is 'explanation', the second is 'story'. The myths of Ancient Greece began as explanations of how the world began and how things became as they did. Stories soon grew around the explanations to make them memorable.

One of the most well-known stories is that of the first woman in the world, the beautiful Pandora. Her name, Pandora, means 'all-gifted' because of the great gifts such as beauty and charm given to her by the gods.

The story begins right back at the beginning of time when there was nothing. No Earth, no sky, no sea; no sun, no moon, no night, no day. The tiniest specks of life swirled in an endless chaotic dance, like dust particles in sunlight. Then shapes began to appear as the larger specks rose upwards and the heavier specks sank down.

The specks of life shifted and changed but
slowly settled to form Mother Earth, called
Gaia and the sky, called Uranus. Together,
Gaia and Uranus created the first rulers
of the Earth – gigantic gods called
the Titans, who in turn gave birth
to a higher race of gods.

But the Titans and gods soon began to argue
with each other. The gods, led by Zeus, forced
the Titans to the furthest ends of the Earth,
and made themselves a new home on
Mount Olympus. Here Zeus took on the
role of master of the world.

Prometheus was a Titan, but the gods liked him and allowed him to roam the Earth and skies freely. One day, he dug up some clay from the ground and began to shape it into tiny statues.

The goddess Athene
was so delighted
with the statues
that she breathed
life into them.
They began to
scuttle about
around Prometheus's
feet like little
matchstick men.

Prometheus was thrilled with his creation. When Mother Earth gave him a sack of gifts to divide among all her living creatures, he let his brother, Epimetheus, share them out. Epimetheus had great fun giving the elephant its trunk, the wasp its sting and the crab its shell.

He gave cunning to the fox, speed to the cheetah and agility to the monkey.

But soon the sack was empty and he had nothing left for Prometheus's little men.

Prometheus was devastated.
'Fool!' he cried. 'Do you never think ahead?'

He watched his tiny naked beings scurrying to and fro with no idea how to feed themselves and keep warm.

'I must do something or they'll die,' he thought.

With that, Prometheus wrapped himself in a cloak of shadows and set off on a terrifying mission: to steal fire from the gods. He made his way to the forge on Mount Olympus, seized a burning coal and escaped, unseen.

The gift of fire changed the life of mankind. With the heat and light it gave them, they could make tools, cook food, hunt and build homes. From the small spark of knowledge it lit, they soon developed a thousand skills. The men were happy in their earthly paradise.

When he saw what had happened, Zeus was livid. 'How dare they steal the secrets of the gods!' he raged. 'I will make them regret the day they were born.'

And so Zeus created Pandora. 'She will be so perfect that no one will be able to resist her,' he said to the other gods. One by one they gave her the gifts of beauty, grace and charm; energy, wit and passion; tenderness, charity and faithfulness.

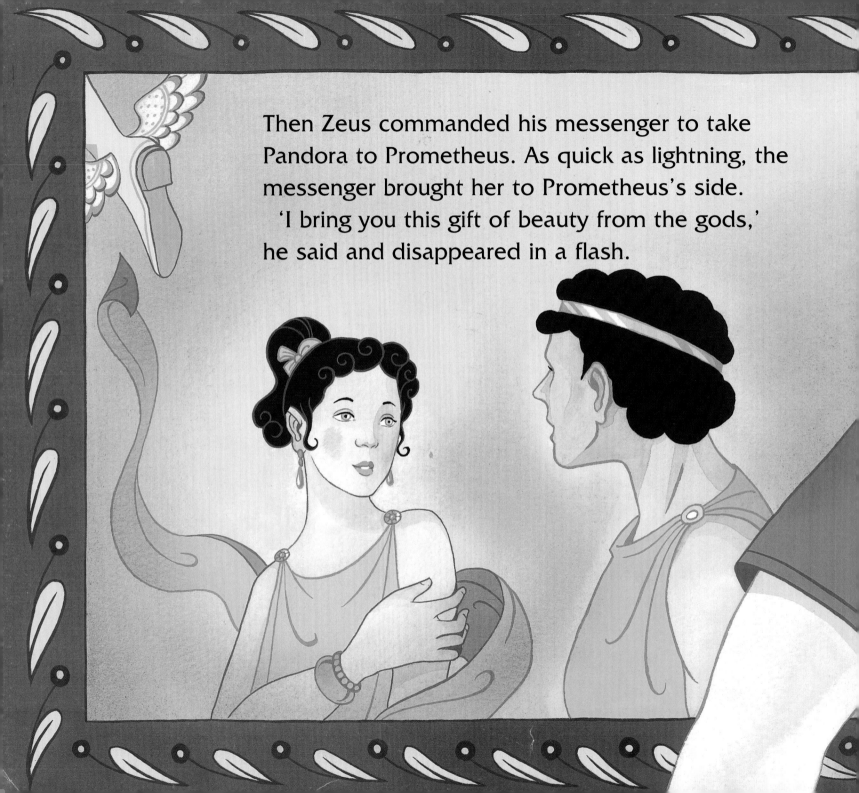

Then Zeus commanded his messenger to take Pandora to Prometheus. As quick as lightning, the messenger brought her to Prometheus's side.

'I bring you this gift of beauty from the gods,' he said and disappeared in a flash.

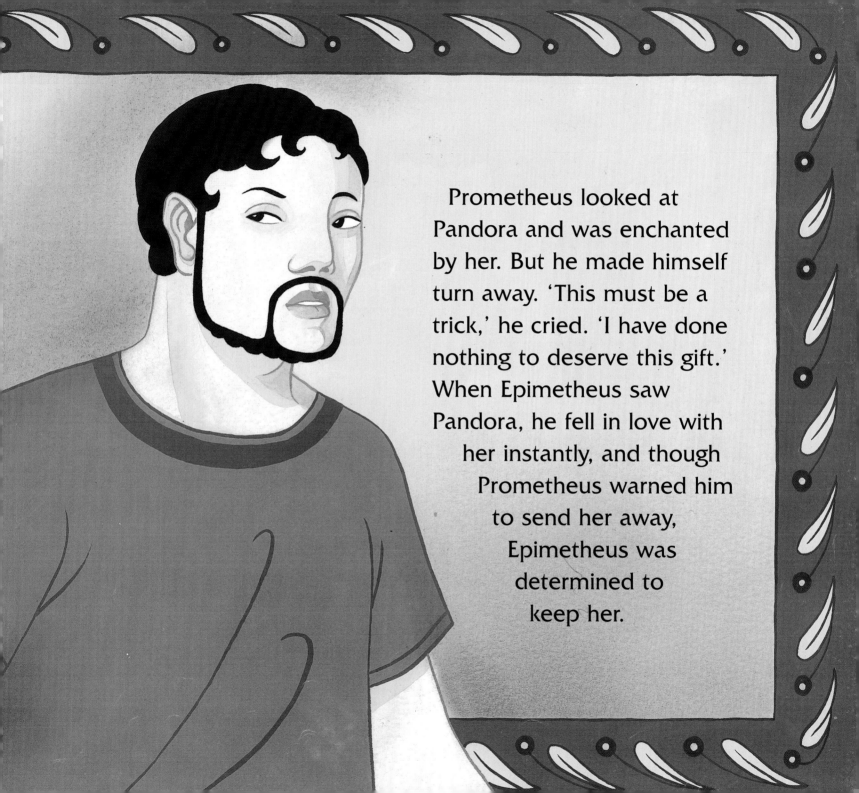

Prometheus looked at Pandora and was enchanted by her. But he made himself turn away. 'This must be a trick,' he cried. 'I have done nothing to deserve this gift.' When Epimetheus saw Pandora, he fell in love with her instantly, and though Prometheus warned him to send her away, Epimetheus was determined to keep her.

Epimetheus and Pandora spent their first days together like two love birds, never leaving each other's side and enjoying life as though they had never experienced it before.

Then one evening, the messenger arrived carrying a heavy box. 'Could I leave this with you?' he asked. 'It's weighing me down and I have work to do.' Epimetheus was only too happy to help. 'I'll collect it shortly,' said the messenger, 'but whatever you do, don't open it.'

Pandora was filled with curiosity. As soon as the messenger had gone she asked, 'What do you think is in it? Can't we have a look?'
 'Good gracious, no,' said Epimetheus. 'It isn't ours to open.' But when Epimetheus left her on her own, Pandora went to the box and ran her fingers over it.

She thought she heard whispers coming from inside the box. 'A little peep wouldn't do any harm,' she thought to herself. 'If I'm quick, no one will ever know,' she decided. And with that she opened the lid.

WHOOOOSH! Thousands of tiny creatures flew into the room, hissing and spitting. They stung Pandora, then bit Epimetheus as he came back into the room.

'What have you done?' he screamed at Pandora as the creatures whirred out of the house and stung every human they encountered.

For the first time in their lives Pandora and
Epimetheus felt pain. For the first time ever they
felt anger and sadness; fear and despair.

Pandora wept at the evil she had let loose on mankind. But Epimetheus thought he heard a voice. He peered into the box.

Trapped in the corner, a tiny creature was calling, 'Set me free and I will heal your wounds.'

Epimetheus carefully freed the creature. It danced round the room, then it fluttered out of the window and lightly touched every human being it met. This tiny creature was Hope. Its mission was to heal the damage caused by all the evil spirits. For wherever there was Hope, there was the possibility of happiness.

ITALY

GREECE

Black Sea

TURKEY

Mediterranean Sea

CRETE

CYPRUS

SYRIA

IRAQ

N

EGYPT

ARABIA

Red Sea

Ancient Greek Empire
(Around 325BC, as conquered
by Alexander the Great, one of the
world's most famous generals.)

Mount Olympus

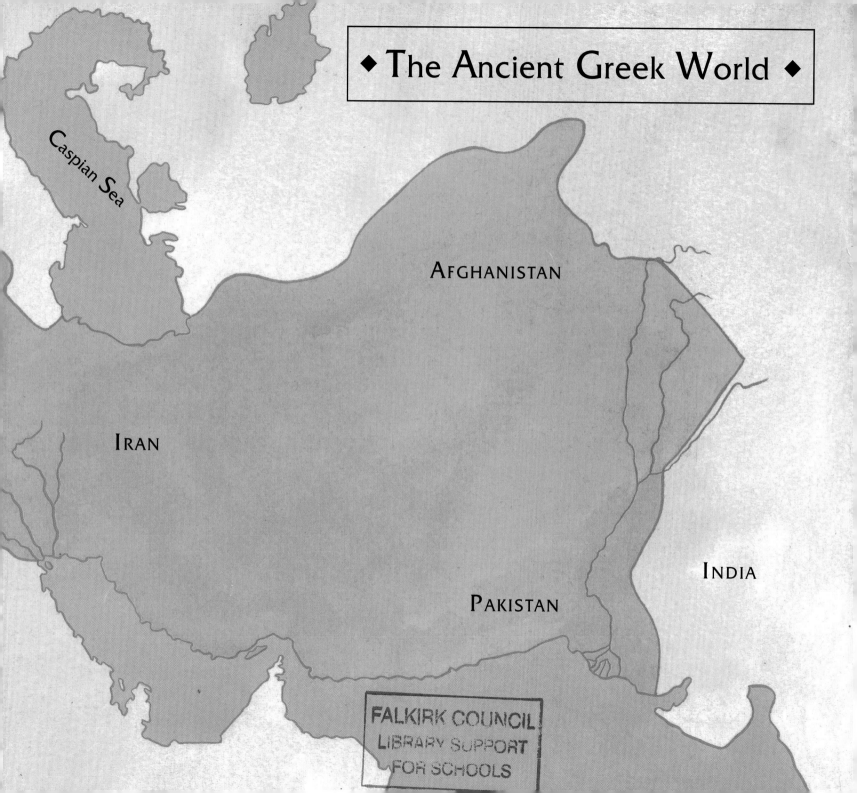

◆ The Ancient Greek World ◆

Caspian Sea

AFGHANISTAN

IRAN

INDIA

PAKISTAN

FALKIRK COUNCIL
LIBRARY SUPPORT
FOR SCHOOLS